For James and Benjamin xx
– L.R.

For Angus Jeremiah Hood
– B.M.

First published 2021 by Macmillan Children's Books
an imprint of Pan Macmillan
The Smithson, 6 Briset Street, London, EC1M 5NR
Associated companies throughout the world
www.panmacmillan.com

ISBN 978-1-5290-0365-9 (HB)
ISBN 978-1-5290-0366-6 (PB)

Text copyright © Lucy Rowland 2021
Illustrations copyright © Ben Rowland 2021

1 3 5 7 9 8 6 4 2

A CIP catalogue record for this book is available from the British Library.

Printed in China

MIX
Paper from
responsible sources
FSC® C116313
FSC
www.fsc.org

Written by

Lucy Rowland

Illustrated by

Ben Mantle

The Three Little Pigs and the Big Bad Book

MACMILLAN CHILDREN'S BOOKS

Ben was a boy who liked stories at night.
A good bedtime tale made everything right.
Stories of knights and of horses that leap,
of wizards and fairies, they helped Ben to sleep.

'The Three Little Pigs' was his best one of all!
'Til the night that some rather strange guests came to call!

They'd got to page seven,
or maybe page six?
Two pigs had built houses
of straw and of sticks.

The third little pig
was all ready to go,
when Mum's mobile rang
in her office below.

Ben's mum said, "Oh dear!
Now who could that be?
I won't be a minute,
I'd better go see."

Ben patiently waited,
"I can't sleep!" he said.
He waited some more
as he wriggled in bed.

"This story's not finished.
We're not half way through!
I'll read it myself,
that's the best thing to do."
But Ben found the words
weren't exactly behaving . . .

Then, outside the window, he saw someone waving!

"Hello!" said a pig, as he clambered right in
(and scratched at the hairs on his chinny chin chin),
"I'm sorry to bother you, really I am,
but I'm finding myself in a bit of a jam.

This story's not finished!" the little pig squeaked.
"And I won't get to sleep now until it's complete."

Ben told him what happened
and showed him the book.
Pig number one was
just having a look,

When outside the window,
well! Who should Ben see?
But Pig number two and
then Pig number three!

The second pig said, "I've a house made of sticks.
But what about him? All he has are some bricks!
Our houses are ready but what about his?
This story's not done. We can't sleep 'til it is!"

Ben said, "I can't read it –
the words are all squiggly."

The second pig said,
"Yes, indeed! Far too wiggly!"

"I've not got my glasses,
you see," said the third.
"Without them, I'm sorry,
I can't read a word."

They started to argue and Ben felt quite glum.
He stared at the pages. Oh where was his mum?

"That's that!" said the first pig.
"We're stuck on page seven!"

His eyes grew quite wide as
he found . . . page eleven!

"The WOLF!" they all gasped and they suddenly knew
that it wouldn't be long until he'd be here too!
Just then came a creak from the old garden gate.
"Uh oh!" said the third pig. "I think we're too late!"

"Little Pigs!" the wolf bellowed.
"Please may I come in?"

"No! Not by the hairs
on our chinny chin chins!"

The pigs grunted down,
"You're not coming inside!"
"But I'd like to be friends now,"
the sorry wolf sighed.

"Go away!" the pigs squealed. "We're not coming down!"
The wolf huffed and puffed, and soon started to frown.

Then, he spotted the chimney . . .
His old favourite trick!

The pigs had a plan,
"Ben, we need a pot, quick!"

They hurriedly set up their trap in the kitchen,
while inside the chimney, the wolf's nose was twitchin'.

He sighed to himself,
"Oh, I've been here before!"
Then he shouted,
"This ending again, are you sure?

I'm ever so tired of
playing this game!"
He called to the pigs,
"Don't you feel the same?"

"Perhaps . . ." the wolf panted,
"If I make amends,
then maybe, instead,
we could try being friends?"

"Friends?" the pigs asked,
as the wolf lost his grip.

"Friends!"
cried the wolf,
as he started to slip!

The wolf toppled down. Yes, he skidded and stumbled.
"That pot will be hot!" howled the wolf as he tumbled.

He took a deep breath and he curled up his feet.
Then he fell with a . . .

. . . BOING! on a soft cotton sheet!
The three little pigs asked him, "Are you alright?"
"I'm fine!" said the wolf (though he'd had quite a fright!)

Just then came a voice saying, "Bye!" from the hall.
At last! Mum had finished her telephone call!

Ben hugged his book tight. He was pleased as could be,
as he looked from the wolf to pigs one, two and three.
This story was finished! And now, time for bed!
. . . or time for one very last story instead?